Pig, Pig, and Pig

The classic story of
The Three Little Pigs

retold by Karin Fisher
illustrations by Karin Fisher

for students at the end of Level 3
of the

International Standard Book Number: 0-9744343-0-2

There are many more stand-alone books available
for the Barton Reading and Spelling System.

To see their titles, or to order them

- Use the order form in the back of this book

- Go to www.BartonReading.com, click on the
  Order button and select Stand Alone Books

- Or call (408) 559-3652

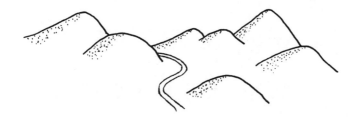

In a snug hut, in a
vast land, Mom Pig
had a small pig child.
It was a soft, pink
ball. Then she had a
next pig, and a next.
"I will call them Pig
One, Next Pig, and

Last Pig," she said
in bliss.

She fed them well
and they got big.

Mom Pig told
them of a dog. "He is
big and bad, and he
has a bad stench. We
call him Big Bad. He
is fond of fresh pig.
To him, all you are is
lunch. When you

have a hut, you must
not let him in."

"Yes, Mom Pig,"
said Pig One.

"We won't let him
in," said Next Pig.

"Thank you for
the tip," said Last Pig.

"You will do well,"
said Mom Pig with a
small sob.

Last Pig said, "Mom

Pig, are you sad?"

"Yes," she said.

Last Pig had a hunch. (He was quick.) He said, "We are big and old. We must split."

"Yes." Mom Pig said with a small, glum nod.

Then she fed them a big pot of hot

slop. And with a kiss, a kiss, and a kiss, she said, "I wish you luck! Do well!" And off went Pig One, Next Pig, and Last Pig, up the big, long path, off to the vast land.

Pig One, Next Pig, and Last Pig went and went and went.

When they got to a big hill, Pig One said, "That is a swell spot. I will have a hut there—a hut of grass."

"Grass?" said
Next Pig and Last Pig.

"Yes, grass," said
Pig One. "I will pack
it with a bit of mud."

And with a kiss
and a kiss, Pig One
said, "I wish you
luck! Do well!" And
off went Next Pig
and Last Pig up the
big, long path.

When Pig One was
done with his grass
hut, he got in his
soft, grass bed to rest.

Just then, Big
Bad, who was on a
hunt for lunch, crept
past the grass hut.
He had a whiff of the
hut. He could smell
pig! "There's a pig
in that shack," he

said. "Yum! I will have fresh ham for lunch." A drop of spit fell from his fang to his chin.

In the grass hut, Pig One could smell a stench. In front of his hut was a dog. Pig One could tell that the dog was big and bad. It was Big Bad!

Big Bad struck the wall of the hut and said, "Pig! I want in!"

"I will not let you in!" said Pig One.

This did not stop Big Bad. The dog said, "Then I'll huff and I'll puff, and I'll bust up your hut!" And he did.

But when Pig One

smelt the stench of
the huff and felt the
gust of the puff, he
fled. He ran up the
big, long path as fast
as a pig can.

Pig One ran and
ran. And there was
Next Pig, who was
just done with his
hut. It was a stick
and twig hut.

"Next Pig!" Pig
One said with a

pant, "Big Bad was at
the grass hut! With
his huff and puff!
The hut is a mess
of grass!"

Next Pig said,
"You sit in this stick
and twig hut. We'll
have a swig of slop
drink and sit on
that log and rest."
And they did.

But Big Bad, who
did not find Pig One
in the mess of grass,
went up the big, long
path, too. He got to
the stick and twig
hut. With a sniff and
a whiff, he could smell
a pig and a pig! "Yum,
yum!" he said. "I will
have a big lunch."

Big Bad struck

the wall of the hut
and said, "Pig and
pig! I want in!"

"We will not let
you in!" said Next
Pig. (Pig One hid.)

"Then I'll huff and
I'll puff and I'll bust
up your hut!" said
Big Bad. And he did.

But when Pig One
and Next Pig smelt

the stench of the huff
and felt the gust of
the puff, they fled.
They ran up the big,
long path as fast as a
pig and a pig can.

Pig One and Next
Pig ran and ran.
And there was Last
Pig, who was just
done with his hut. It
was a swell hut of
strong brick.

"Last Pig!" Next

Pig said with a pant, "Big Bad was at the stick and twig hut! With his huff and puff! The hut is a mess of stick and twig!"

"And he was at the grass hut!" said Pig One, "It is a mess of grass!"

Last Pig said, "You sit in this

strong brick hut.
We'll have a mud
bath in that big brick
tub and rest." And
they did.

But Big Bad, who
did not find Pig One
and Next Pig in the
mess of stick and
twig, went up the
big, long path, too.
He was mad.

Big Bad got to the
brick hut. With a
whiff and a sniff and
a sniff again, he
could smell a pig, a
pig, and a pig! Then
he was not mad.
"Yum, yum, yum!" he
said. "I will have a
big, grand lunch."

Big Bad struck
the wall of the hut

and said, "Pig, pig, and pig! I want in!"

"We will not let you in!" said Last Pig. (Pig One and Next Pig hid.)

"Then I'll huff and I'll puff and I'll bust up your hut!" said Big Bad. But he didn't. He did huff, and he did puff, but the brick was strong. The hut did not fall. There was not one crack in any wall.

"Scram, Big Bad!" said Pig One, Next Pig, and Last Pig with a grin, a grin, and a grin.

Then Last Pig said to Pig One and Next Pig, "This hut is

big. We can all have
this strong brick hut."

"Yes!" said Pig One

"Thank you!" said
Next Pig.

"Let's all have a
big slop sandwich!"
said Last Pig.

"Yum! Yum! Yum!"
said pig, pig, and pig.

Big Bad slunk off.
He went back to his

den where he had an
old can of ham and a
bit of crust for lunch.
And he did not huff
and puff at the brick
hut again.

Like this Book?

There are additional titles available from the Barton Reading & Spelling System. See the order form in the back of this book.

**Known Syllable Types
at the end of Level 3
of the Barton Reading
& Spelling System:**
Closed Syllables
Unit Syllables
Contractions

**Known High Frequency Sight
Words used in this book:**
a, are, could, do, done, he, have,
one, said, the, there, they, was,
we, who

**Unknown High Frequency
Sight Words used in this book:**
sandwich

The Barton Reading and Spelling System

It's the fastest way to become a great tutor because all the training and materials you need come inside each level.

Just watch our tutor training videos on a Saturday afternoon and start tutoring on Monday! The Orton-Gillingham-based system that we feature is exactly what research demonstrates works best for people with dyslexia.

Yet we designed our videos so that parents, volunteers in early intervention programs, and new private tutors can quickly "get it" and succeed.

In fact, thousands already have.

To learn more, visit www.BartonReading.com

Or call 408-559-3652 and ask for our FREE Demonstration video.

☐ Yes, send me your most recent list of titles.
☐ Yes, send me the titles selected below right now.

Titles for students at the end of Level 3 include:

A Job for Jeff *by Peggy Smith* . . . . $7.95 _____

Fish, Fox, and Then Some *by Karin Fisher*. $7.95 _____

Pig, Pig, and Pig *by Karin Fisher* . . . . $7.95 _____

The Champ *by Peggy Smith* . . . . $7.95 _____

The Quest *by Andra Hansen* . . . . $7.95 _____

The Tax Man *by Andra Hansen* . . . . $7.95 _____

Subtotal _____

California residents add sales tax _____

Total _____

Name: _____

Organization: _____

Address: _____

City, State, Zip: _____

Phone: ( )_____

Email: _____

Payment Method

☐ Check enclosed *(made out to Bright Solutions for Dyslexia, Inc.)*

☐ Purchase Order enclosed

☐ Visa/MC #:_____
    Expires:_____

mail or fax this order form to
Barton Reading & Spelling System
2059 Camden Avenue, Suite 186 • San Jose, CA 95124
Phone: (408) 559-3652 • Fax: (408) 377-0503
Email: info@BrightSolutions.US